Reading.

It takes you places.

www.greaterhartfordreads.org

Literacy
Council

860.522.READ (7323)

Disney's

Pooh's Magic Wishes

Adapted by Amy Edgar

Based on the screenplay by Mark Zaslove

Photography by John Barrett

Disney
PRESS

New York

Special thanks to: Shadow Projects, Shadow Character Design, and Shadow Digital

Designed by Charles Kreloff

Copyright © 2001 by Disney Enterprises, Inc.

Based on the Pooh stories by A. A. Milne (copyright The Pooh Properties Trust).

Printed in the United States of America

First Edition

Library of Congress Card Number: 2001090380

ISBN 0-7868-3345-9

For more Disney Press fun, visit www.disneybooks.com

Fun with **Pooh's Magic Wishes!**

Pooh's Magic Wishes makes learning to read fun! Your child will enjoy chanting Pooh's magical wishing rhyme, featured on every other page.

Here are some ways for your child to learn and have fun while reading **Pooh's Magic Wishes** with you!

Find Pooh's wishing rhyme.

First, look through the book to find Pooh's wishing rhyme. Just look for Pooh's picture above it and lots of wishing stars around it. Each time it appears it's your child's turn to read!

Say the rhyme together.

Read the rhyme to your child first. Then say it together a few times until your child is able to repeat it along with you.

Take turns reading!

You read the story. Your child "reads" the rhyme. Your child may need help at first, but before the story is over, your child will be "reading" it independently!

Deep in the Hundred-Acre Wood, it was spring. To Rabbit, it was time for spring cleaning.

Tigger wanted to help. "I'll jump on this board to get rid of all these honey-pots. I spring, and all's clean!" he said.

"I didn't mean *that* kind of spring!" said Rabbit.

Not far away, Pooh was taking a walk and wishing out loud for some honey.

"I'm wishing once.
I'm wishing twice.
I'm wishing hard
for something nice."

Just then a honeypot fell from the sky and landed right in front of him.

"Hmmm," said Pooh. "Maybe my wishing is working. Let me try that again."

"I'm wishing once.
I'm wishing twice.
I'm wishing hard
for something nice."

Thunk! A second honeypot landed at Pooh's feet.

"When I rhyme, my wishes come true!" Pooh told Piglet. "All I have to say is . . .

"I'm wishing once.
I'm wishing twice.
I'm wishing hard
for something nice."

"I am the Great Pooh-dini," said Pooh. And I want to share my wishes with my friends."

Rabbit wished for a carrot as big as a tree. Tigger wished he could bounce up to the moon. Piglet wished to spend some time with his best friend.

Pooh said his rhyme.

"I'm wishing once.
I'm wishing twice.
I'm wishing hard
for something nice."

"Prepare to have your wishes granted," announced the Great Pooh-dini.

Pooh imagined Rabbit in his garden with a carrot as big as a tree. Then, he repeated his magical rhyme.

"I'm wishing once.
I'm wishing twice.
I'm wishing hard
for something nice."

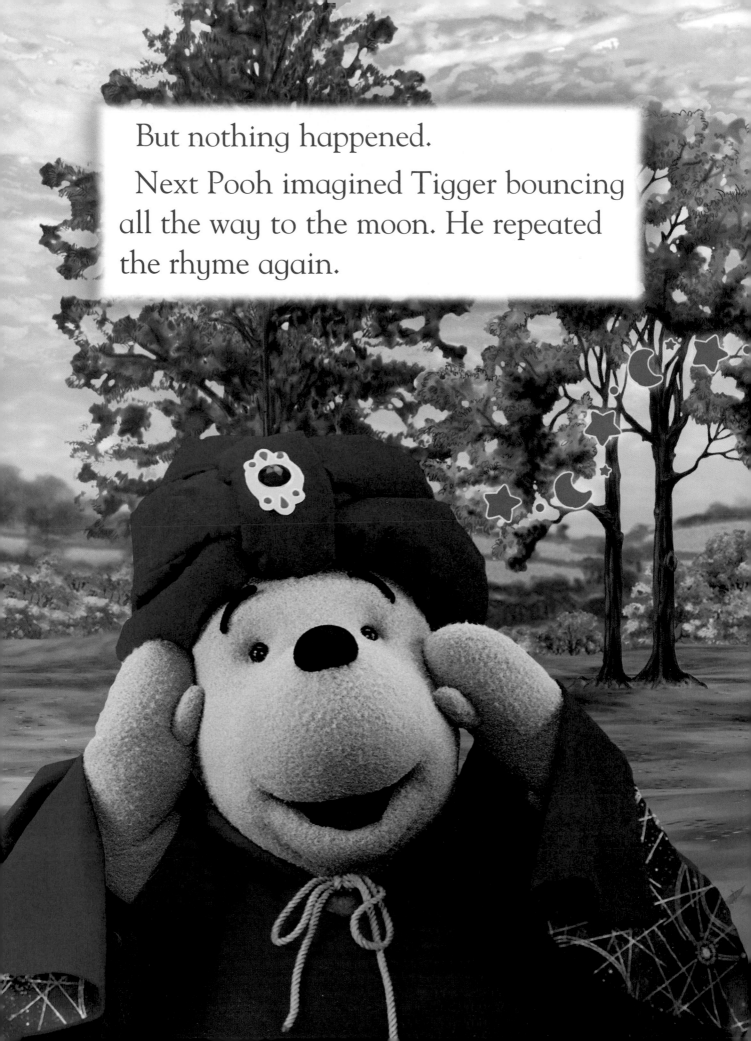

But nothing happened.

Next Pooh imagined Tigger bouncing all the way to the moon. He repeated the rhyme again.

"I'm wishing once.
I'm wishing twice.
I'm wishing hard
for something nice."

Hmmm . . . nothing happened this time, either. They waited and waited.

"I guess my magical wishing rhyme isn't working anymore," Pooh said sadly.

Tigger and Rabbit went home.

Pooh tried again.

"I'm wishing once.
I'm wishing twice.
I'm wishing hard
for something nice."

Still, nothing happened.

"I disappointed our friends," said Pooh. "I couldn't grant their wishes."

"Pooh," said Piglet, "the best wishes are inside your heart."

Pooh brightened. "You've given me an idea, Piglet," he said. He said his magical wishing rhyme once more for good luck.

"I'm wishing once.
I'm wishing twice.
I'm wishing hard
for something nice."

And then he went right to work.

"We'll surprise Rabbit by weeding his garden," said Pooh. "That will make his carrots grow."

And he began his rhyme again.

"I'm wishing once.
I'm wishing twice.
I'm wishing hard
for something nice."

"With this telescope, Tigger will feel like he's closer to the moon," said Pooh.

"Good idea," said Piglet.

Pooh smiled and said his rhyme again.

"I'm wishing once.
I'm wishing twice.
I'm wishing hard
for something nice."

The next morning Rabbit discovered his whole garden had been weeded. And Tigger found the brand-new telescope.

Pooh had made his friends so happy! And all it took was a little hard work and his magic rhyme.

"I'm wishing once.
I'm wishing twice.
I'm wishing hard
for something nice."

But then Pooh turned to Piglet. "I didn't do anything nice for *you*," he said.

"My wish came true exactly," said Piglet. "I got to spend time with my very best friend."

Then they all said the rhyme together.

"I'm wishing once.
I'm wishing twice.
I'm wishing hard
for something nice."

My friends and I made some very special wishes—and so can you! Don't forget my magical wishing rhyme. Use it whenever you want to make a special wish!

"I'm wishing once.
I'm wishing twice.
I'm wishing hard
for something nice."

More Fun with
Pooh's Magic Wishes!

Turn the tables!

After reading the story a few times, change roles! You read the wishing rhyme and invite your child to be the storyteller. Your child will have fun recalling the events of the story and hearing you say the rhyme.

If I was the Great Pooh-dini…

Help your child copy Pooh's wishing poem on a large sheet of paper, then draw pictures of all of the things he or she would make come true!

Make rhyming wishes.

Have fun making up your own rhyming wishes! Challenge your child to come up with rhymes that rhyme with one you start. You might begin with: "I'm wishing for a hat." See how many rhyming wishes your child can think of, such as "I'm wishing for a cat," "I'm wishing for a bat," and so on.